LOST IN THE FOURTH DIMENSION

Jonathan Litton

Quarto is the authority on a wide range of topics.

Quarto educates, entertains and enriches the lives of our readers—enthusiasts and lovers of hands-on living.

www.quartoknows.com

Author: Jonathan Litton
Illustrator: Sam LeDoyen
Consultants: Hilary Koll & Steve Mills
Editor: Amanda Askew
Designer: Punch Bowl Design
QED Editor: Carly Madden

First published in the UK in 2017 by
QED Publishing
Part of The Quarto Group
The Old Brewery
6 Blundell Street
London, N7 9BH

A catalogue record for this book is available from the British Library.

ISBN 978-1-78493-854-3

Printed in China

MIX
Paper from
responsible sources
FSC® C016973

HOW TO BEGIN YOUR ADVENTURE

Are you ready for a brain-bending mission packed with puzzles and problems?

Then this is the book for you!

Lost in the Fourth Dimension isn't like other books where you read through the pages in order. It's a lot more exciting than that because you're the main person in the story! You have to find your own way through the book, flicking backwards and forwards, following the clues until you've finished the whole adventure.

The story starts on page 4, and then tells you where to go next. Every time you face a challenge, you'll have a choice of answers, which look something like this:

A If you think the correct answer is A, GO TO PAGE 23

B If you think the correct answer is B, GO TO PAGE 11

Choose the correct answer, and then find the correct page and look for the icon.

Don't worry if you pick the wrong answer. You'll be given an extra clue, then you can go back and try again.

The puzzles and problems in *Lost in the Fourth Dimension* are all about the wonderful world of measurements.

To help you there's a list of useful words at the back of the book, starting on page 44.

Are you ready?

Then turn the page and let's get started!

LOST in the FOURTH DIMENSION

FLASH!

You are woken by a flash of light as your spaceship tunnels through a wormhole!

With a splutter and a bang, the engine stops. You have no idea where you are or how to get home...

To get back to Earth safely, you'll need to think on your feet. **GET GOING ON PAGE 19.**

Right! Watts are standard units of power. You press the button and the spaceship jumps into life for a few seconds... then fails!

Oh no! You need a jumpstart of power from the fuelling station, but you don't have any money left.

You explain your situation to the owner and he suggests a gamble...

If you can answer this question correctly, you can have a free jumpstart. If not, I keep your ship.

He asks: All of these units are used for length... except for one. Which is the odd one out?

Megametre.
TURN TO PAGE 19

Chain.
GO TO PAGE 39

Cubic metre.
JUMP TO PAGE 10

No, 7 x 5 litres = 35 litres.
GO BACK AND
TRY AGAIN ON PAGE 10.

Wrong! That's 4 hours and 30 minutes from now.
HAVE ANOTHER TRY ON PAGE 39.

That's right! 2 x 324 = 648. The portal opens up and you step through it.

A

Alien A.
GO TO PAGE 10

You land on a planet teeming with aliens of all shapes and sizes – most of them look pretty fierce! You check the map for clues.

Trust the beast who's 12 "feet" tall. Forget the rest – avoid them all!

Measure each alien's height using the length of one of their feet as the **base unit**. Good luck!

B

Alien B.
FLIP TO PAGE 38

Without being noticed, measure each alien's foot. Which alien is 12 feet tall?

C
Alien C.
HEAD TO PAGE 27

D
Alien D.
JUMP TO PAGE 19

HINT: Use a finger to measure each alien's foot size and then see how many times this measurement goes into their height.

Correct! The green path avoids the alien and covers a distance of 26 intergalactic units, which you calculated by adding the numbers together.

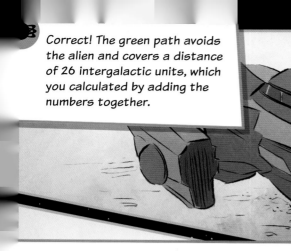

Your decision-making was good, but your steering was terrible – you've crash-landed!

Fortunately, you know the SOS symbol – a **rectangle** with its long sides twice as long as its short sides. You lay out a 4-m length of rope as one side of the rectangle.

Which length of rope should you select to complete the symbol?

8 metres.
GO TO PAGE 34

18 metres.
HEAD TO PAGE 21

22 metres.
TURN TO PAGE 30

You turn the key but the engine stays silent. Although the perimeter is 12, the area of this key is 7.
HAVE ANOTHER GO ON PAGE 19 BEFORE IT'S TOO LATE!

Wrong answer – the bottle of water is too light. Try converting all the weights into zilograms.
HAVE ANOTHER TRY ON PAGE 30.

30° Correct! You set the controls to 30 **degrees** and zoom towards the purple planet with ease.

As you're about to touch down on the surface of the purple planet, a man waves urgently at you.

Could you hover for another 25 **seconds** before landing?

Your landing clock says 12H 34M 56S. What time should you set it to?

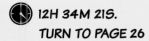 12H 34M 21S.
TURN TO PAGE 26

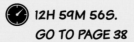 12H 59M 56S.
GO TO PAGE 38

 12H 35M 21S.
JUMP TO PAGE 32

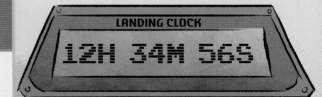

LANDING CLOCK
12H 34M 56S

5 No! The trees appear twice as big, but the distance has halved.
TRY AGAIN ON PAGE 11.

0.3 No. 0.3 written as a **fraction** would be 1/3. You need to **divide** 1 in half.
TRY AGAIN ON PAGE 23.

D

Yes, the key fits! The key has 12 units around the edge (perimeter) and contains six **squares** (area). The spacecraft's engine hums into life.

Oh no! Now the cooling system alarm is beeping. The control panel says you need to add 40 **litres** of water. You go to the storage area.

You have 5-litre water bottles.

COOLING SYSTEM

BEEP! BEEP! BEEP!

How many bottles should you add?

 6.
TURN TO PAGE 39

 8.
GO ON TO PAGE 29

 7.
OVER TO PAGE 5

Correct. A **cubic metre** is a measure of **volume** rather than length. The owner is cross, but lets you use the horsepower machine.

You need 1500 Watts to get going.

2

1   **3**

1 HORSEPOWER EQUALS 750 WATTS

How many horsepower should you set the machine to give your spaceship?

 One horsepower.
GO TO PAGE 41

 Two horsepower.
OVER TO PAGE 22

 Three horsepower.
ZOOM TO PAGE 33

A

No, this alien is not to be trusted – he's smaller than 12 feet tall.
TRY AGAIN ON PAGE 6 BEFORE HE NOTICES YOU! ◉

Well done! By following 2 km S, 3 km E, you reach the forest.

Just as you approach the trees, aliens carry a giant magnifying glass past you, which makes everything appear twice as big as it really is.

Through the magnifying glass, the trees look like they are 10 metres away, but how far are they really?

 5 metres. FLIP TO PAGE 9

 20 metres. TURN TO PAGE 42

12

Correct. There are 12 inches in a foot.
A foot is just over 30 centimetres.

Excellent!
Greetings, Earthling!

I have a map that will
help you, if you can answer
this final question...

...there are 3.2 feet
in 1 **metre**. How many feet
are there in 9 metres?

What do you say?

✖
32.5.
OVER TO PAGE 26

◆
28.8.
ZOOM TO PAGE 39

▲
27.
JUMP TO PAGE 18

Earth is small, but not as tiny as
2500 miles in circumference.
TRY AGAIN ON PAGE 32
BEFORE HE TURNS HIS BACK ON YOU.

No, travelling the full diameter
would take you to the other side
of the galaxy.
TRY AGAIN ON PAGE 38. **0.5**

That's right! 5 x 5 zongs is 25. The officer mutters that you're quicker at maths than driving!

Hmmm, I'm still concerned that you don't know about speeds – and if so, I'll confiscate this spacecraft.

Answer this: If you drive at a speed of 5 zongs per ding-dong for 9 ding-dongs, how many zongs will you travel?

What do you answer?

40 40.
FLIP TO PAGE 21

45 45.
JUMP TO PAGE 43

55 55.
TURN TO PAGE 33

No, the bridge is not yet level because the book is too light. Convert everything into zilograms to find the right answer.
GO BACK TO PAGE 30.

1

No, that tree has 18 squares, which is not a square number.
TRY AGAIN ON PAGE 42.

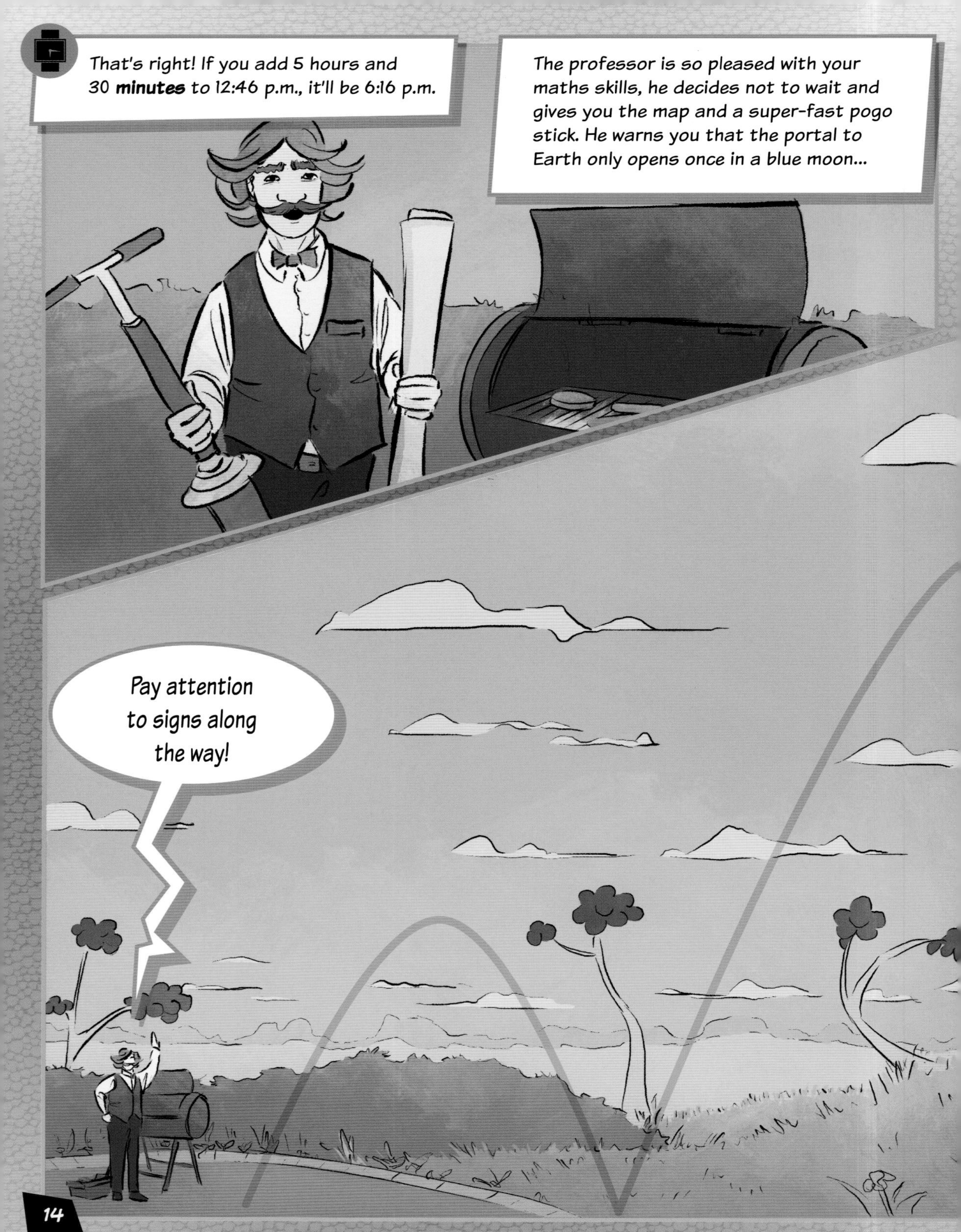

That's right! If you add 5 hours and 30 **minutes** to 12:46 p.m., it'll be 6:16 p.m.
The professor is so pleased with your maths skills, he decides not to wait and gives you the map and a super-fast pogo stick. He warns you that the portal to Earth only opens once in a blue moon...
Pay attention to signs along the way!

From the map you learn that there is a password-controlled portal at the north pole of the planet.

You start pogoing from the equator, and pass a sign showing the distance to the pole — not long to go!

324 miles to the pole

GET THERE QUICKLY ON PAGE 30.

12ℓ Well done! You hand over your money and load up with 12 litres of fuel before getting ready to leave.

click! click! click!

Unfortunately your 'new' spaceship is even older than the professor, and needs some brute force to get the engine started!

HEAVE HO, 1500 UNITS OF POWER WILL MAKE ME GO!

PRESS THE BUTTON THAT SHOWS A UNIT OF POWER TO GET A KICKSTART.

WATTS   VOLTS   LUMENS

Which button shows a unit of power?

 Watts.
JUMP TO PAGE 5

 Volts.
GO TO PAGE 18

 Lumens.
FLIP TO PAGE 37

90° No, 90 degrees would take you straight up, away from any of the planets, and towards a deadly black hole!
QUICKLY RETHINK ON PAGE 43.

No, the portal stays shut. You haven't doubled the number of the sign correctly.
HAVE ANOTHER TRY ON PAGE 37.

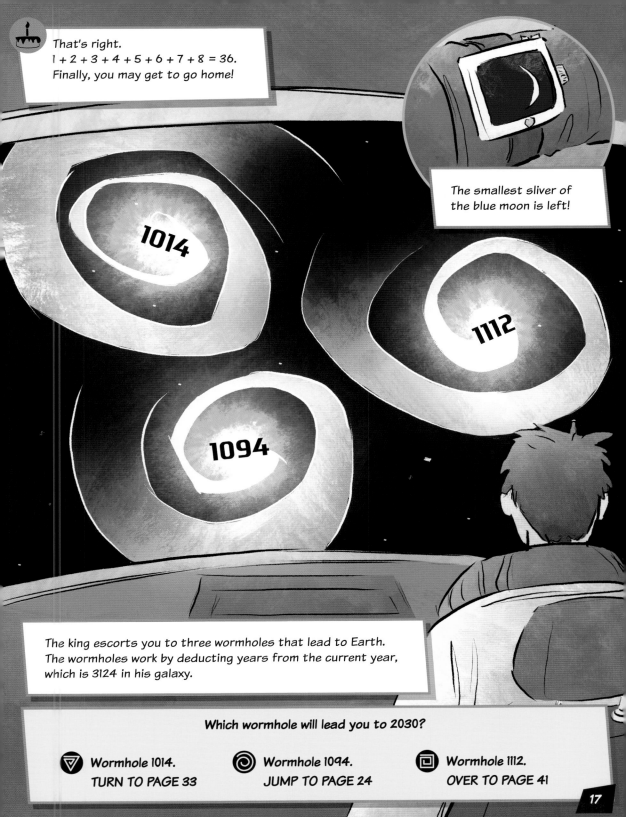

That's right.
$1 + 2 + 3 + 4 + 5 + 6 + 7 + 8 = 36$.
Finally, you may get to go home!

The smallest sliver of the blue moon is left!

1014

1112

1094

The king escorts you to three wormholes that lead to Earth. The wormholes work by deducting years from the current year, which is 3124 in his galaxy.

Which wormhole will lead you to 2030?

Wormhole 1014.
TURN TO PAGE 33

Wormhole 1094.
JUMP TO PAGE 24

Wormhole 1112.
OVER TO PAGE 41

Approximately 25,000 miles is correct. The professor smiles and asks his second question eagerly.

Question two: how long, approximately, is the Amazon River in miles?

Hmmm, I know that the longest river, the Nile, is more than 4000 miles long, so how long is the Amazon River?

What do you answer?

499 miles.
HEAD TO PAGE 30

4000 miles.
JUMP TO PAGE 36

60,000 miles.
FLIP TO PAGE 20

Nice try. You get 27 if you multiply 9 by 3, but you need to multiply by 3.2.
HAVE ANOTHER TRY ON PAGE 12. 12

Afraid not. Volts are the unit of electrical force rather than power.
TRY AGAIN ON PAGE 16. 120

You begin to feel light-headed – the oxygen must be running out. Next to the control panel is a glass box labelled SMASH IN AN EMERGENCY. This definitely counts!

There are five small, differently shaped keys inside the box. You read the instructions – choose quickly!

CRACK!

If you get into a fix, choose an ignition key to over-ride the system and start the engine.
IGNITION KEY: Perimeter = 8 + 4 and Area = 6.

A
B
C
D
E

Which is the correct key?	**A** A. TURN TO PAGE 8	**B** B. JUMP TO PAGE 37	**C** C. FLIP TO PAGE 23	**D** D. GO TO PAGE 10	**E** E. HEAD TO PAGE 42

D

Watch out! This alien isn't 12 feet tall and looks like it may have spotted you.
TRY AGAIN ON PAGE 6.

No, a megametre is a very big unit of measure, equal to a million metres.
TRY AGAIN ON PAGE 5.

2 Correct! 9 is a square number. You scale the tree's branches and take a bite from the juiciest piece of fruit you can find.

Suddenly, the scenery transforms – the tree becomes a spaceship, and the forest becomes an intergalactic refuelling station. You're saved!

FLASH!

You have 6 intergalactic dollars. Fuel is usually priced at 1 dollar per litre, but today there is a half-price sale. What luck!

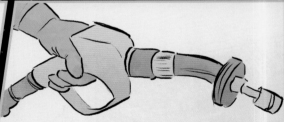

How much fuel can you buy?

3 litres.
GO TO PAGE 36

9 litres.
FLIP TO PAGE 31

12 litres.
HEAD TO PAGE 16

30 zongs per ding-dong would be 6 x 5 zongs and that's a bit too fast.
TRY AGAIN ON PAGE 29.

60,000 miles is far too long. The professor looks at you with doubt.
GET THE ANSWER RIGHT ON PAGE 18.

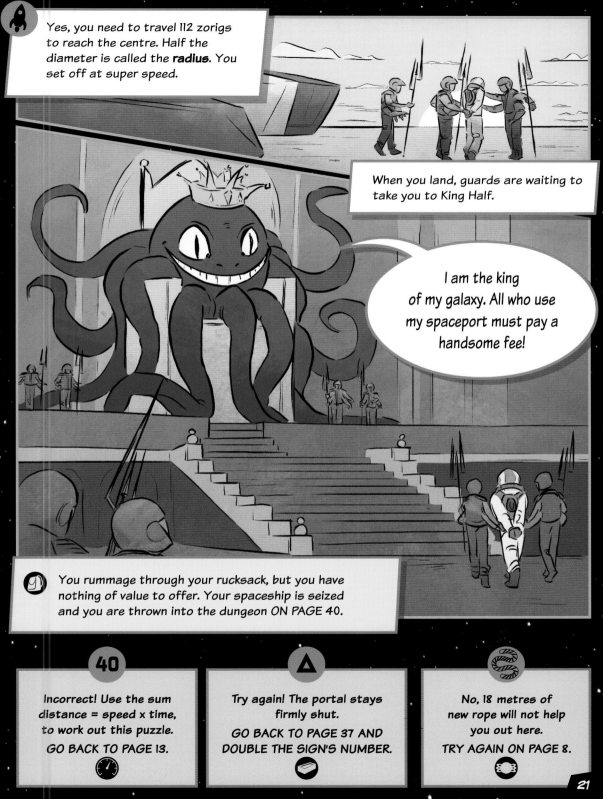

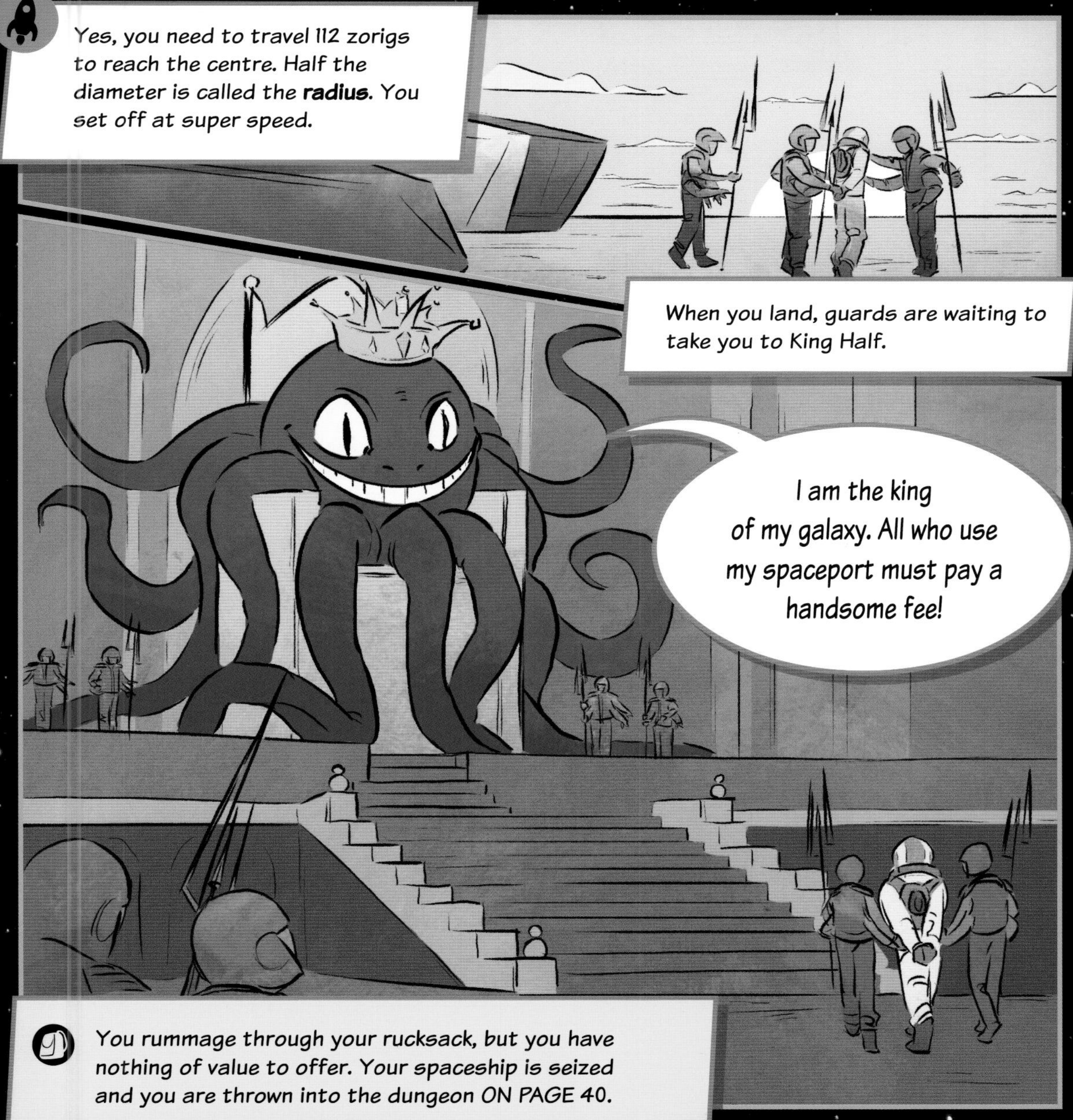
Yes, you need to travel 112 zorigs to reach the centre. Half the diameter is called the **radius**. You set off at super speed.
When you land, guards are waiting to take you to King Half.
I am the king of my galaxy. All who use my spaceport must pay a handsome fee!
You rummage through your rucksack, but you have nothing of value to offer. Your spaceship is seized and you are thrown into the dungeon ON PAGE 40.

40

Incorrect! Use the sum distance = speed x time, to work out this puzzle.

GO BACK TO PAGE 13.

Try again! The portal stays firmly shut.

GO BACK TO PAGE 37 AND DOUBLE THE SIGN'S NUMBER.

No, 18 metres of new rope will not help you out here.

TRY AGAIN ON PAGE 8.

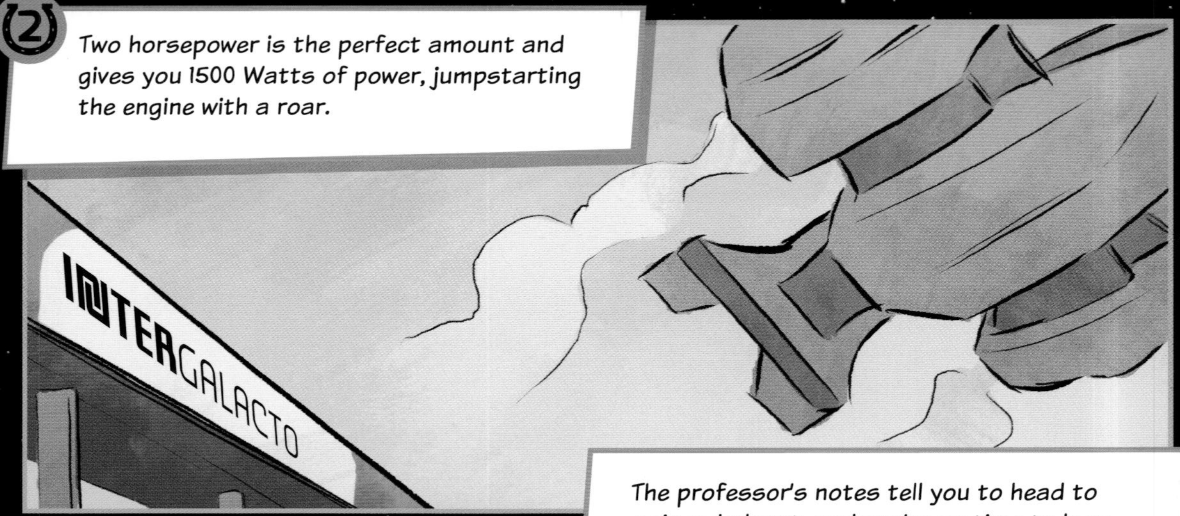
Two horsepower is the perfect amount and gives you 1500 Watts of power, jumpstarting the engine with a roar.
INTERGALACTO

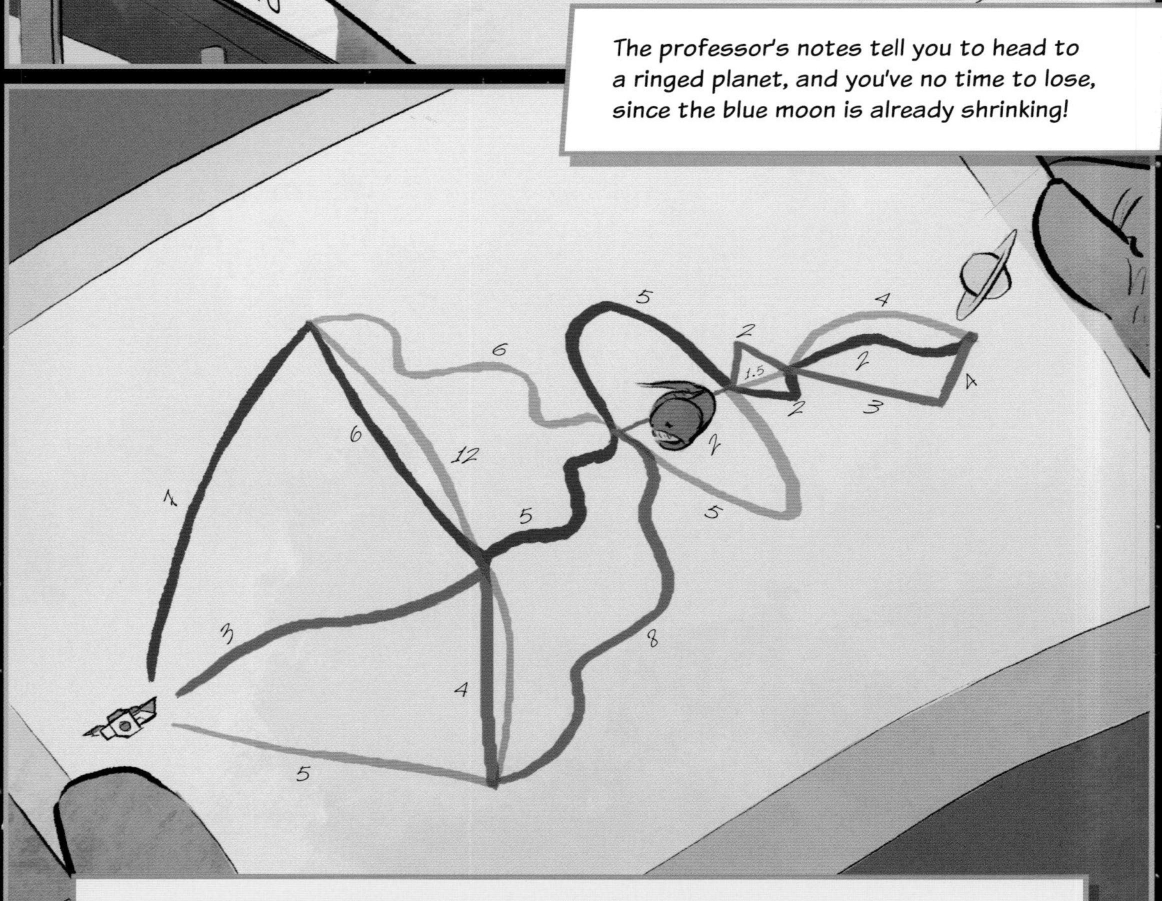
The professor's notes tell you to head to a ringed planet, and you've no time to lose, since the blue moon is already shrinking!

You sketch possible routes. Which path is the shortest route that will get you there while avoiding the unfriendly alien?

Blue path.
HEAD TO PAGE 38

Orange path.
JUMP TO PAGE 28

Green path.
TURN TO PAGE 8

Correct. At 2 km/h, it'll take them 3 hours to reach you and, by then, you'll be long gone.

With your spaceship fixed, the owner offers to make you a drink. When he goes inside, you blast off!

King Half Spaceport

HALF IS INVALID.
ENTER AS
A **DECIMAL**.

Looking closely at the map, you spot a huge spaceport. Perhaps someone there can help you find your way back to Earth.

You type in 'King Half' on your computerised mapping system to get directions.

What is 'half' as a **decimal**?

0.3 0.3. *GO TO PAGE 9*

1.5 1.5. JUMP TO PAGE 43

0.5 0.5. HEAD FOR PAGE 38

C The only sound is of your breathing, which is getting more strained. The key didn't start the engine because it only has an area of 4!
PICK AGAIN ON PAGE 19.

10 No, an inch is just over 2.5 centimetres, and a foot is just over 30 centimetres. The calculation you need is 30 ÷ 2.5 = ?.
THINK AGAIN ON PAGE 36.

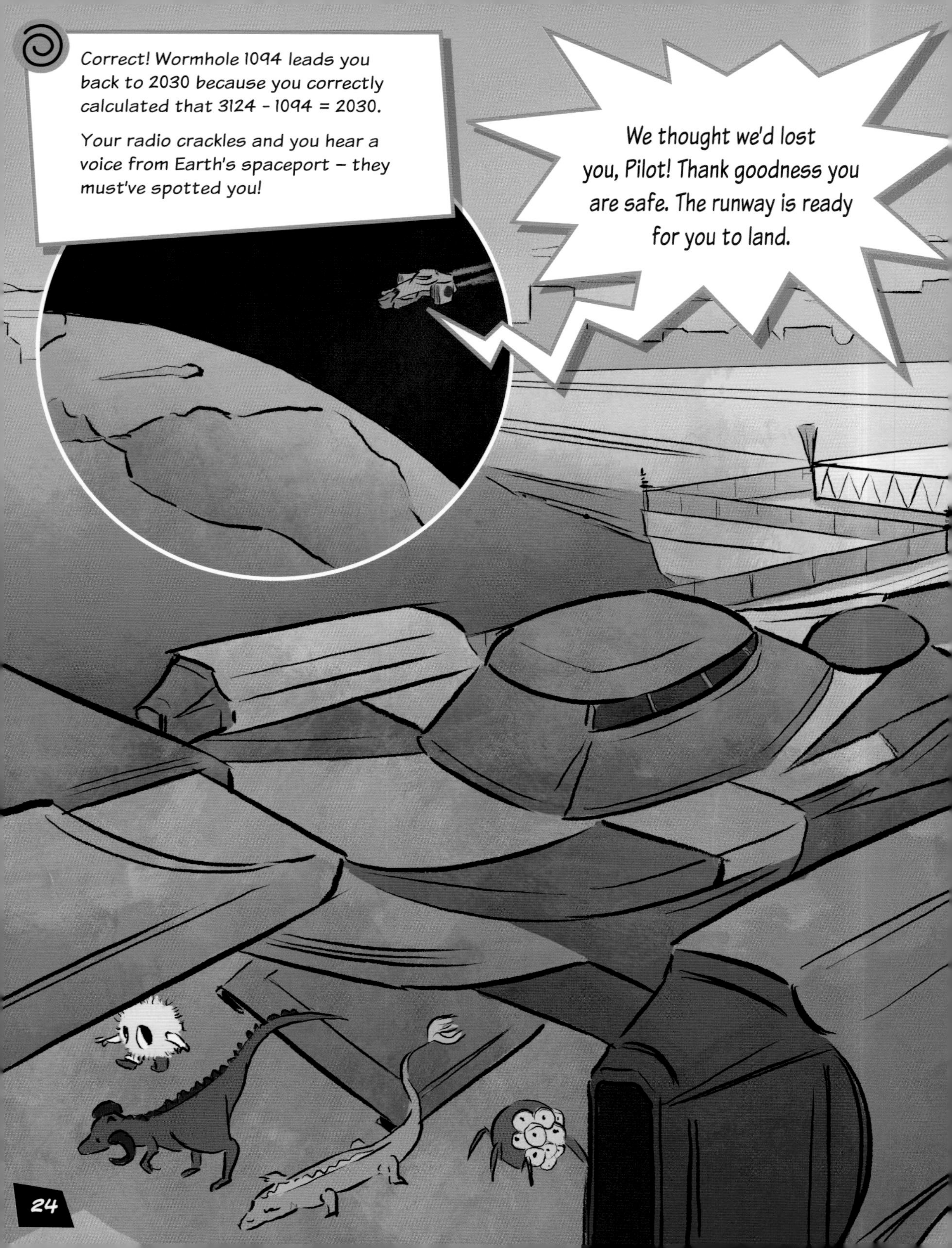
Correct! Wormhole 1094 leads you back to 2030 because you correctly calculated that 3124 - 1094 = 2030.
Your radio crackles and you hear a voice from Earth's spaceport – they must've spotted you!
We thought we'd lost you, Pilot! Thank goodness you are safe. The runway is ready for you to land.

Congratulations, you land back on Earth with a bump! A crowd greets you, waving flags and cheering! Your commander praises your intelligence and gives you a week off. Result!

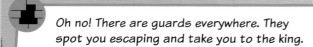

Oh no! There are guards everywhere. They spot you escaping and take you to the king.

You explain that you came to the spaceport in the hope that the king might know the way back to Earth.

Ok, if you can answer my puzzle, I'll lead you home. If not, you will become my entertainer.

Nine lives have I;
Eight have passed,
each one longer than the last.
My first was just one year long,
then two, three, four, and so on.
My ninth begins this very day...
How old am I,
what do you say?

Quick, answer before he changes his mind!

 36 years old.
ZOOM TO PAGE 17

 45 years old.
HEAD TO PAGE 43

 54 years old.
OFF TO PAGE 28

 If the clock reads 12H 34M 21S, you'd have gone back in time.
SET THE CORRECT TIME ON PAGE 9. 30°

 Incorrect. You need to multiply 3.2 by 9 to get the correct answer.
GO BACK TO PAGE 12.

 No, if they walk, they'll be with you in 2 hours — there's a slower way.
TRY AGAIN ON PAGE 35.

26

C

Correct! If you measure carefully, this alien is about 12 feet tall, so must be friendly. You slowly approach...

Hello there. The professor sent me here to find the route to a forest portal. I need to get there quickly. Do you know the way?

Sort of, but my route is a bit long-winded.

If you can simplify my **directions**, you'll reach the forest in no time!

The alien tells you this route:
5 km N, 3 km W, 7 km S, 5 km E, 1 km S, 1.5 km E, 1 km N, 0.5 km W

Clue: Think of North and South first and then East and West separately.

You are here ✗

Which route should you take?

↵ 6 km S, 3 km W. GO TO PAGE 33

↳ 2 km S, 3 km E. ZOOM TO PAGE 11

↱ 5 km N, 0.5 km E. OVER TO PAGE 41

At 45 degrees, you'd be close, but headed for the yellow planet.
LOOK CLOSELY ON PAGE 43.

45°

33.3 cm is a little too long. The longest possible length of a SHORT is just under 50 cm, and the shortest possible SHORT is just above 0 cm.
USE THIS TO FIND THE AVERAGE ON PAGE 40.

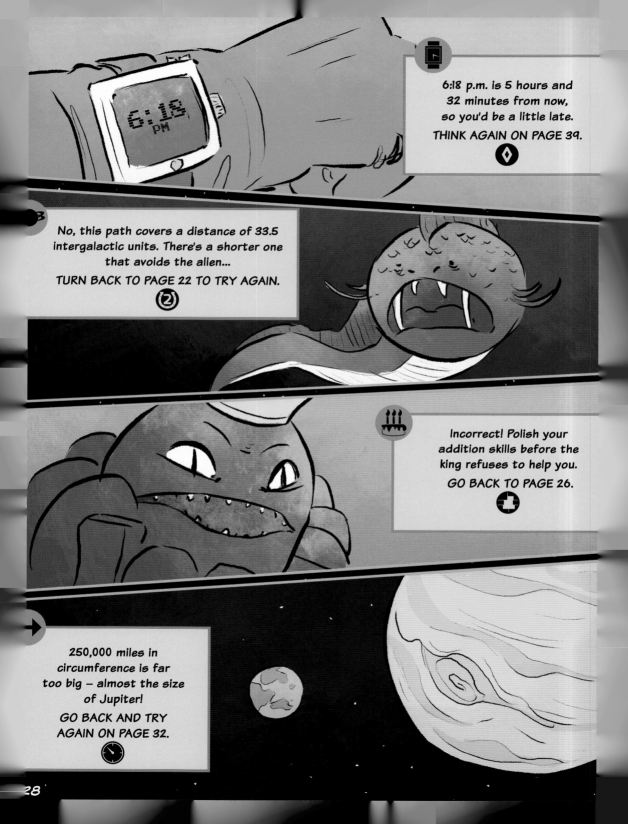

6:18 p.m. is 5 hours and 32 minutes from now, so you'd be a little late.
THINK AGAIN ON PAGE 39.

No, this path covers a distance of 33.5 intergalactic units. There's a shorter one that avoids the alien...
TURN BACK TO PAGE 22 TO TRY AGAIN.

Incorrect! Polish your addition skills before the king refuses to help you.
GO BACK TO PAGE 26.

250,000 miles in circumference is far too big — almost the size of Jupiter!
GO BACK AND TRY AGAIN ON PAGE 32.

8 8 is right! 8 x 5 litres = 40 litres.

Finally, your spacecraft is functioning well. As you steady the steering, you see a flashing blue light and hear a CLUNK – the police are boarding your ship!

Greetings. Did you realize you covered the last 5 zongs in 1 ding-dong?

Sorry, officer. I didn't know I was going so fast.

Fast? You're travelling so slowly that you're causing a traffic jam. The minimum **speed** here is 5 times that! How many zongs per ding-dong is that?

Work this one out quickly – he looks cross! What do you say?

 20.
FLIP TO PAGE 41

 25.
TURN TO PAGE 13

 30.
GO TO PAGE 20

You're nearly at the portal when you come across a bridge.

It's kept in place using suspended **weights**, but one of the weights is missing.

You'll need to balance the bridge by adding weight. The bridge weights are in zilograms, whereas the objects you have in your rucksack are in **kilograms**.

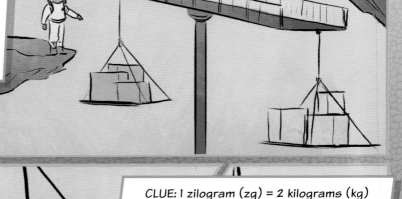

1 kg

4 kg

0.5 kg

CLUE: 1 zilogram (zg) = 2 kilograms (kg)

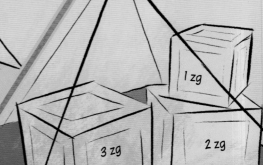

1 zg

1 zg

1 zg

0.5 zg

0.5 zg

3 zg

2 zg

1 zg

Which object will balance the bridge so you can cross?

 Bottle of water.
GO TO PAGE 8

 Brick.
JUMP TO PAGE 37

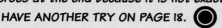 **Book.**
HEAD TO PAGE 13

 No, 499 miles isn't long enough. Also, an approximate answer would usually leave zeroes at the end because it is not exact.
HAVE ANOTHER TRY ON PAGE 18.

No, with another 22 metres of rope, you'll make a symbol that no one will recognize.
TRY AGAIN ON PAGE 8.

Yes! The SHORT pieces have random lengths between 0 cm and 50 cm, so the average length will be around 25 cm.

The blue moon is just a sliver now.

Mincent shows you a secret exit, and you sneak out of the dungeon TO PAGE 26.

No, an inch is just over 2.5 centimetres, and a foot is just over 30 centimetres.
THINK ABOUT THE CALCULATION YOU NEED TO USE ON PAGE 36.

6

Try again! 9 litres isn't right. The new price is half a dollar per litre — how many half dollars are there in 6 dollars?
TRY AGAIN ON PAGE 20.

2

Great! You set the landing clock to 12H 35M 21S and touch down without a hitch.

Thanks – you cooked my sausages super-quick! Professor Inchington-Smythe is the name and maths puzzles are my game! I come from a land you've probably never heard of, called Earth.

Perfect! You explain what's happened and ask if he can help you find your way back home.

He agrees to help you – but only if you can prove you're from Earth. He challenges you to three maths puzzles that only a true Earthling could answer.

Question one: what is the **circumference** of Earth... in miles?

What do you say?

← 2500 miles. TURN TO PAGE 12

● 25,000 miles. GO TO PAGE 18

→ 250,000 miles. HOP OVER TO PAGE 28

No, 3124 – 1014 will take you to 2110.
HAVE ANOTHER TRY ON PAGE 17.

55

55 is too far! Try using the equation distance = speed x time.
WORK OUT THE ANSWER ON PAGE 13.

Danger! wasteland

Oh no! That's far too much horsepower and may break your spaceship once and for all.
GO BACK TO PAGE 10.

Oh dear, you've strayed off course following 6 km S, 3 km W. Look at N and S first and then E and W.
TRY AGAIN ON PAGE 27.

Correct. With 8 metres of rope you can make another long side of 4 metres and two short sides of 2 metres.

Soon enough, a tow-ship arrives from a local comet and takes you to a garage.

WE LOVE HUMANS

HUMANS ROCK

WE LOVE HUMANS

WE LOVE HUMANS

The garage owner tells you that he's part of a WE LOVE HUMANS club and that the other members would love to head back to your spaceship for selfies. You don't have time for this – the blue moon is getting smaller.

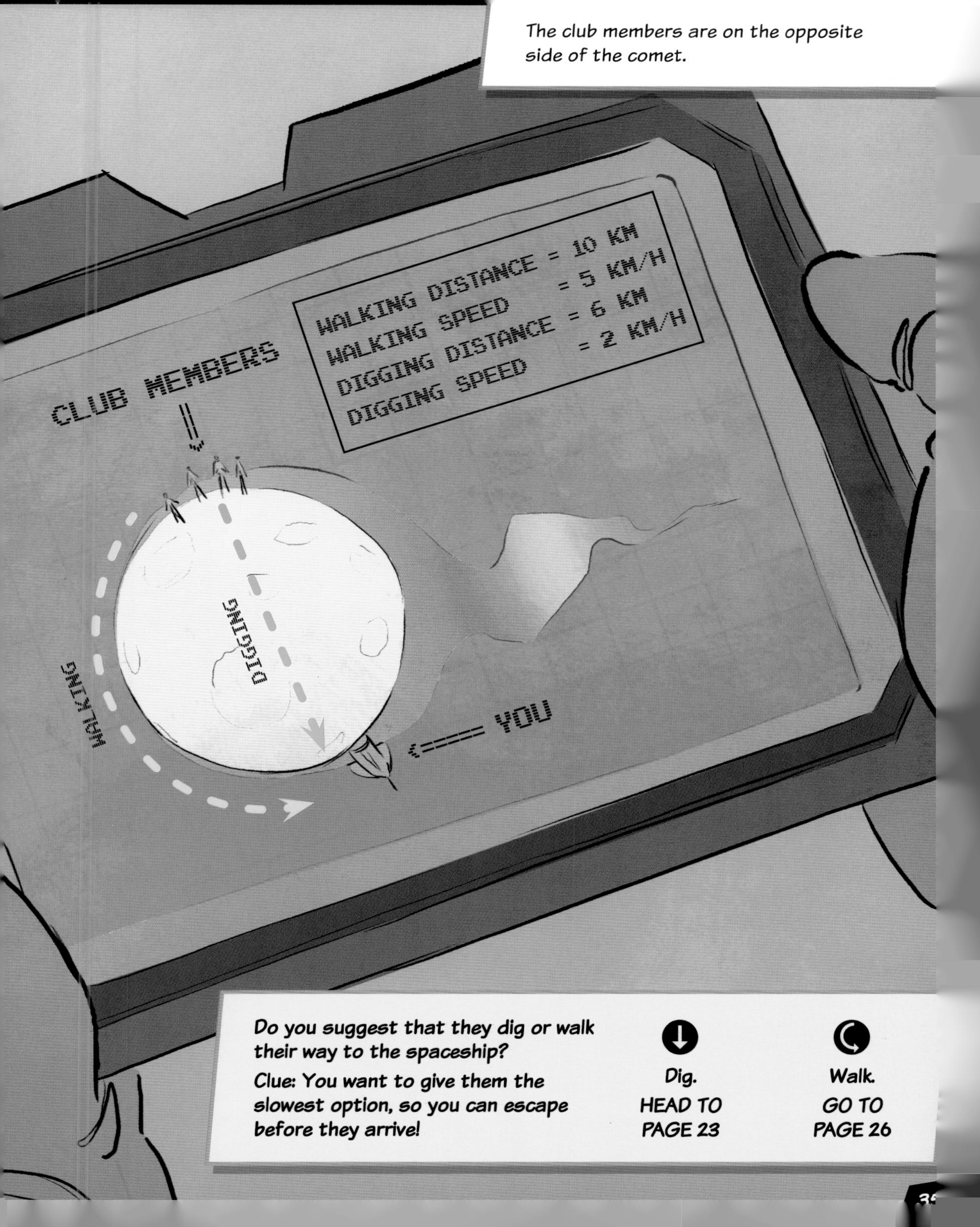
The club members are on the opposite side of the comet.
WALKING DISTANCE = 10 KM
WALKING SPEED = 5 KM/H
DIGGING DISTANCE = 6 KM
DIGGING SPEED = 2 KM/H
CLUB MEMBERS
DIGGING
WALKING
<==== YOU

Do you suggest that they dig or walk their way to the spaceship?

Clue: You want to give them the slowest option, so you can escape before they arrive!

Dig.
HEAD TO PAGE 23

Walk.
GO TO PAGE 26

Approximately 4000 miles is correct. The professor is standing now, his face full of glee.

Question three: how many **inches** are in a **foot**?

What do you say?

6
6 inches.
JUMP TO PAGE 31

10
10 inches.
GO TO PAGE 23

12
12 inches.
HEAD TO PAGE 12

No! That tree has 27 squares, which is not a square number.
GO BACK AND HAVE ANOTHER GO ON PAGE 42.

No, you can buy a lot more than 3 litres. The sale price is half a dollar per litre.
CORRECT YOUR CALCULATION ON PAGE 20.

Correct! You bolt the bridge into place before crossing; otherwise your own weight will undo your clever arithmetic as you cross it!

You reach the portal in no time.

It has a keypad with a clue to the password.

ENTER THE PASSWORD
Double the distance on the signpost you passed on your way here.

No wonder the professor told you to pay attention. What number do you enter?

648.
GO TO PAGE 6

668.
HEAD TO PAGE 16

712.
FLIP TO PAGE 21

B The area of this key is only 5.
PICK AGAIN ON PAGE 19, WHILE YOU STILL CAN!

Try again! Lumens are the unit of brightness, not power.
GO BACK TO PAGE 16.

0.5

Correct! Half written as a decimal is 0.5.

You type in the number and a map appears on the screen. You need to head to the centre of the galaxy.

You are on the outskirts of the galaxy, which is shaped like a circle, and its **diameter** is 224 zorigs.

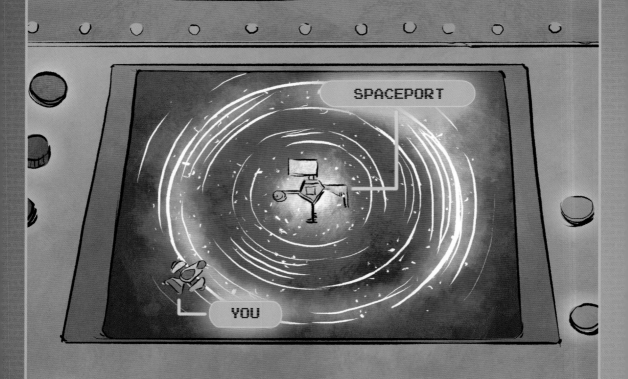

How many zorigs must you travel to get there?

 112 zorigs.
GO TO PAGE 21

 224 zorigs.
OFF TO PAGE 12

If you get to 12H 59M 56S, you've added on 25 minutes rather than 25 seconds.
IF YOU DON'T WANT TO RUN OUT OF POWER, TRY AGAIN ON PAGE 9.

30°

B

No, this alien is shorter than 12 feet tall!
STAY WELL AWAY AND HAVE ANOTHER GO ON PAGE 6.

Incorrect – this path brings you face to face with a hungry flesh-eating alien. Yikes!

TURN AROUND AND TRY AGAIN ON PAGE 22 BEFORE HE GETS ANY CLOSER!

28.8 is right!
3.2 x 9 = 28.8.

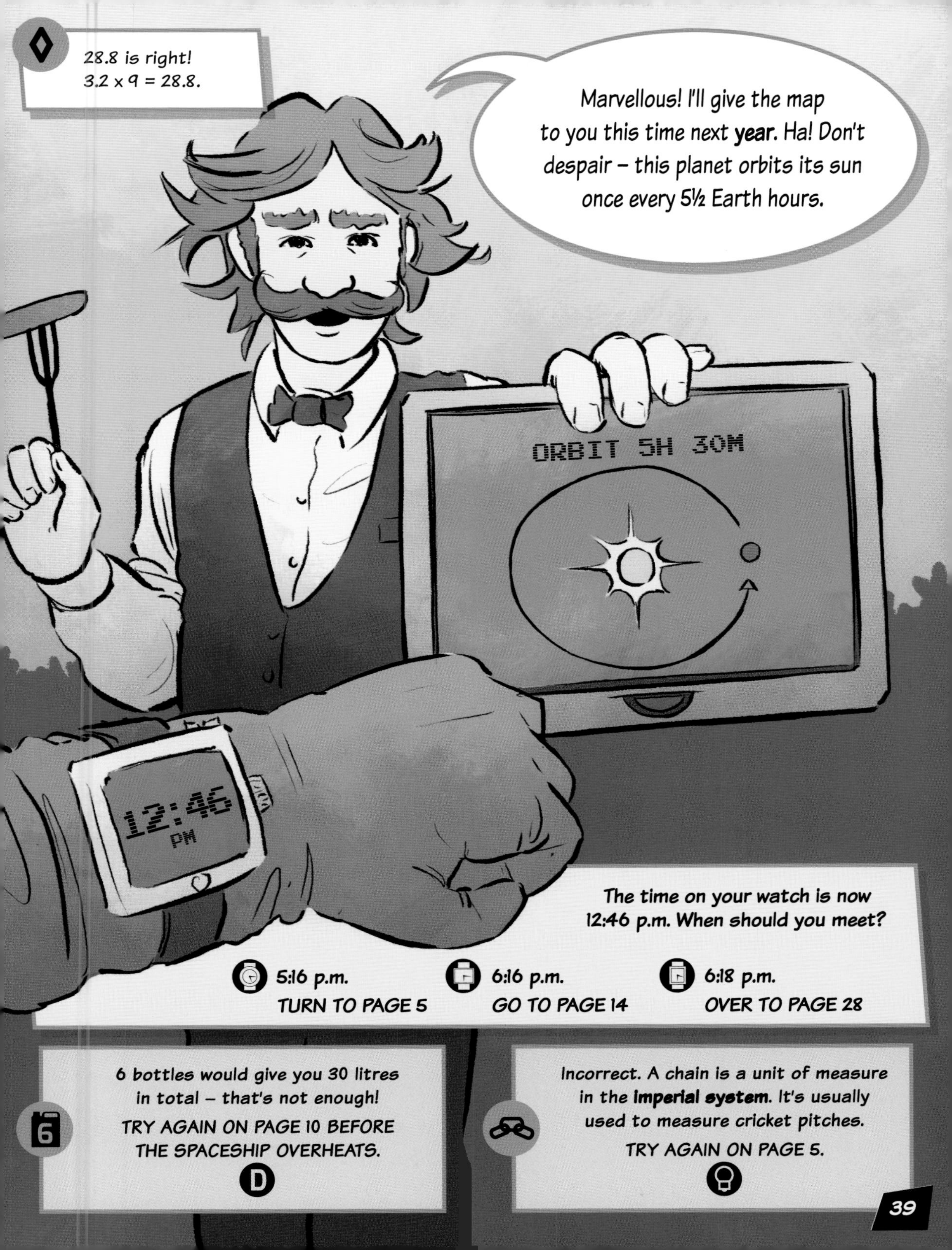
Marvellous! I'll give the map to you this time next **year**. Ha! Don't despair – this planet orbits its sun once every 5½ Earth hours.
ORBIT 5H 30M
12:46
PM

The time on your watch is now 12:46 p.m. When should you meet?

5:16 p.m.
TURN TO PAGE 5

6:16 p.m.
GO TO PAGE 14

6:18 p.m.
OVER TO PAGE 28

6

6 bottles would give you 30 litres in total – that's not enough!

TRY AGAIN ON PAGE 10 BEFORE THE SPACESHIP OVERHEATS.

D

Incorrect. A chain is a unit of measure in the **imperial system**. It's usually used to measure cricket pitches.

TRY AGAIN ON PAGE 5.

In the dungeon, you see a man in a funny costume. You learn that his name is Mincent, the king's ex-entertainer, who was put here for being too boring.

I'd rather be in here than entertaining that oaf. I actually know a way out... King Half created a secret exit, just in case he ever got thrown into his own dungeon!

Let's play a game. If you win, I'll tell you where the exit is. If not, you'll stay here forever!

LONGS

SHORTS

He explains that he spends his days carving metre sticks, then snaps them into two pieces at random. He throws these into two baskets – one labelled LONGS and the other marked SHORTS.

What do you think the average length of the SHORTS is likely to be?

What do you say?

 25.0 cm.
GO TO
PAGE 31

 33.3 cm.
HEAD TO
PAGE 27

 35.0 cm.
JUMP TO
PAGE 42

Incorrect. 3124 – 1112 leads you to 2012, back in time.

QUICKLY CHOOSE THE RIGHT WORMHOLE ON PAGE 17 BEFORE IT'S TOO LATE.

That's not enough power — one horsepower is only 750 Watts.

TRY AGAIN ON PAGE 10.

$$1hp = 750W$$

No, 20 zongs per ding-dong would be 4 x 5 zongs, which is too slow.

PUT YOUR MULTIPLICATION HAT ON TO GET THE RIGHT ANSWER ON PAGE 29.

No, 5 km N, 0.5 km E is not the correct route, so you end up in the middle of Wild Woods.

HOT FOOT IT BACK TO PAGE 27 AND TRY AGAIN.

Danger! Wild Woods

20 Correct! The trees are 20 metres away.

You read the next instruction on the professor's map.

It says to count the blocks on each tree to see which tree represents a **square number**, and then pick fruits from the top of that tree.

HINT: A square number is the number you get when you **multiply** a number by itself, such as $2 \times 2 = 4$ and $3 \times 3 = 9$.

Which tree should you climb?

① Tree 1.
HOP TO PAGE 13

② Tree 2.
OVER TO PAGE 20

③ Tree 3.
GO TO PAGE 36

E The engine remains silent when you turn the key. Make sure you count the squares to find the correct area – the area of this key is 7.

PICK AGAIN ON PAGE 19.

 35.0 cm is too long. The longest possible length of a SHORT is just under 50 cm, and the shortest possible SHORT is just above 0 cm.

THINK AGAIN ON PAGE 40.

45

Exactly right! **Distance** = speed x **time**, and 5 x 9 = 45.

There's hope for you yet. Where are you heading?

I'm trying to find my way back to Earth. Can you help?

No, but I met a man from Earth this morning. He was on that purple planet. Maybe he can help.

He points to your computerised mapping system. You only have a small amount of power left, so you need a direct route.

COMPUTERISED MAPPING SYSTEM

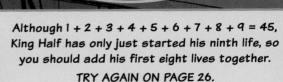

Please enter the required angle to reach the purple planet

What launch angle should you enter on your control system?

30° 30 degrees. GO TO PAGE 9

45° 45 degrees. HEAD TO PAGE 27

90° 90 degrees. FLIP TO PAGE 16

 1.5 No, it would be King One-and-a-Half Spaceport if 1.5 were right.
HAVE ANOTHER GO ON PAGE 23.

 Although 1 + 2 + 3 + 4 + 5 + 6 + 7 + 8 + 9 = 45, King Half has only just started his ninth life, so you should add his first eight lives together.
TRY AGAIN ON PAGE 26.

GLOSSARY

ANGLE
An angle is a measurement of turn. For example, a right angle has 90 degrees.

AREA
The amount of space that a shape covers. It can be measured in cm², m² and km².

BASE UNIT
The starting measurement of something.

CHAIN
A unit of distance, equal to 22 yards. It is usually used to measure cricket pitches.

CIRCUMFERENCE
The distance around the outside of a circle.

CUBIC METRE (M³)
A measure of volume. It can be thought of as a cube that is 1 metre on each side.

DECIMAL
A number that is not a whole number, but has a digit or digits after the decimal point, shown by using tenths, hundredths, and so on. A half or 1/2 is shown as the decimal 0.5.

DEGREE (°)
A unit for measuring the size of an angle. A complete turn (full circle) has 360 degrees. A right angle (quarter turn) has 90 degrees.

DIAMETER
A straight line from one side of a circle to the other side, going through the centre of the circle.

DIRECTION
The way that something or someone is moving or facing.

DISTANCE
The size of the gap between two places or things.

DIVIDE
In a calculation, the dividing sign tells you to divide the first number by the second number to find the answer. Example: 8 ÷ 4 = 2.

FOOT
A unit of length equal to 12 inches or approximately 30 centimetres.

FRACTION
A part of a whole number, such as 1/2 or 3/4.

IMPERIAL SYSTEM
A system of measurement used in the UK and USA, as well as other countries. Units include feet, inches, miles, ounces and pounds.

INCH
A unit of distance, equal to approximately 2.5 centimetres. There are 12 inches in 1 foot.

KILOGRAM (KG)
A unit of weight, equal to 1000 grams.

LITRE (L)
A unit to measure liquid, equal to 1000 millilitres.

METRE (M)
The standard unit of length, equal to 100 centimetres.

MINUTE
A unit of time, equal to 60 seconds.

MULTIPLY
In a calculation, the multiplication or times sign tells you to multiply numbers together to find the answer. Example: 9 x 7 = 63.

PERIMETER
The distance around the outside of a two-dimensional shape.

RADIUS
The distance from the centre to the edge of a circle.

RECTANGLE
A shape that has four straight sides, two of which are longer than the others, and four 90 degree angles at the corners.

SECOND (S)
The standard unit of time. 60 seconds is equal to 1 minute.

SPEED
A measure of how fast an object travels. Speed = distance ÷ time. It is measured in kilometres per hour, miles per hour, metres per second, and so on.

SQUARE
A four-sided shape containing four right angles. The lengths of all sides are the same.

SQUARE NUMBER

If you multiply any number by itself you get a square number. Example: 5 x 5 = 25, so 25 is a square number. If you have a square number of counters, you can always arrange them in a perfect square shape.

TIME

The progression from past to present to future. Measured in seconds, minutes, hours, days, years, and so on.

VOLUME

A measure of how much space a three-dimensional object takes up. The units of volume include cubic metres and cubic centimetres.

WEIGHT

A measure to show how heavy something is.

YEAR

A unit of time, defined as the time it takes for a planet to orbit its sun. An Earth year is approximately 365 days.

TAKING IT FURTHER

The Maths Quest books are designed to motivate children to develop and apply their maths skills through engaging adventure stories. The stories work as games in which children must solve a series of mathematical problems to progress towards the exciting conclusion.

The books do not follow a conventional pattern. The reader is directed to jump forwards and backwards through the book according to the answers given. If their answers are correct, they progress to the next part of the story; if the answer is incorrect, the reader is directed back to try the problem again. Additional support may be found in the glossary at the back of the book.

TO SUPPORT YOUR CHILD'S MATHEMATICAL DEVELOPMENT YOU CAN:

- ∞ Read the book with your child.

- ∞ Solve the initial problems and discover how the book works.

- ∞ Continue reading with your child until he or she is using the book confidently, following the GO TO instructions to find the next puzzle or explanation.

- ∞ Encourage your child to read on alone. Ask 'What's happening now?'. Prompt your child to tell you how the story develops and what problems they have solved.

- ∞ Discuss measurements in everyday contexts: working out how long something is, estimating how many steps it takes to walk somewhere, filling up different-sized containers with water.

- ∞ Have fun with measurements: guess the weight of lots of different objects and then weigh them on some kitchen scales; give them a ruler and ask them to measure the length of objects around the house.

- ∞ Use an analogue clock and a digital clock to tell the time. Make the puzzles harder by asking your child to add a certain amount of time to what is shown.

- ∞ Most of all, make maths fun!